THE Adventures of

CAPTAIN UNDERPANTS

TRA-LA-LAAAA!

A
LITTLE APPLE PAPERBACK

An Epic Novel by

DAV PILKEY

SCHOLASTIC INC.
New York Toronto London Auckland Sydney

For David and Nancy Melton
with gratitude

No part of this publication may be reproduced, stored in a retrieval system,
or transmitted in any form or by any means, electronic, mechanical,
photocopying, recording, or otherwise, without written permission
of the publisher. For information regarding permission, please write to:
Permissions Department, Scholastic Inc., 557 Broadway, New York, NY 10012.

This book is being published simultaneously in hardcover by the Blue Sky Press.

ISBN 978-0-590-84628-8 (Trade) / ISBN 978-0-545-38566-4 (BC)

Copyright © 1997 by Dav Pilkey
All rights reserved. Published by Scholastic Inc.
SCHOLASTIC, THE BLUE SKY PRESS, and associated logos are
trademarks and/or registered trademarks of Scholastic Inc.

Be sure to check out Dav Pilkey's Extra-Crunchy Web Site O' Fun at
www.pilkey.com.

132 131 130 129   18 19 20 21 22 23 24 25 26/0

Printed in the United States of America   40

First Scholastic paperback printing, September 1997

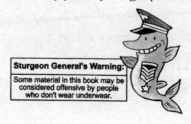

Sturgeon General's Warning:
Some material in this book may be
considered offensive by people
who don't wear underwear.

CHAPTERS

CHAPTER 1
GEORGE AND HAROLD

Meet George Beard and Harold Hutchins. George is the kid on the left with the tie and the flat-top. Harold is the one on the right with the T-shirt and the bad haircut. Remember that now.

George and Harold were best friends.
They had a lot in common. They lived
right next door to each other and they
were both in the same fourth-grade class
at Jerome Horwitz Elementary School.

George and Harold were usually
responsible kids. Whenever anything bad
happened, George and Harold were
usually responsible.

But don't get the wrong idea about these two. George and Harold were actually very nice boys. No matter what everybody else thought, they were good, sweet, and lovable. . . . Well, OK, maybe they weren't so sweet and lovable, but they were good nonetheless.

It's just that George and Harold each had a "silly streak" a *mile* long. Usually that silly streak was hard to control. Sometimes it got them into trouble. And once it got them into big, *BIG* trouble.

But before I can tell you that story, I have to tell you *this* story.

CHAPTER 2

TREE HOUSE COMIX, INC.

After a hard day of cracking jokes, pulling
pranks, and causing mayhem at school,
George and Harold liked to rush to the
old tree house in George's backyard.
Inside the tree house were two big old
fluffy chairs, a table, a cupboard crammed
with junk food, and a padlocked crate
filled with pencils, pens, and stacks and
stacks of paper.

Now, Harold loved to draw, and George loved to make up stories. And together, the two boys spent hours and hours writing and drawing their very own comic books.

Over the years, they had created hundreds of their own comics, starring dozens of their own superheroes. First there was "Dog Man," then came "Timmy the Talking Toilet," and who could forget "The Amazing Cow Lady"?

But the all-time greatest superhero they ever made up *had* to be "The Amazing Captain Underpants."

George came up with the idea.

"Most superheroes *look* like they're flying around in their underwear," he said. "Well, this guy actually *is* flying around in his underwear!"

The two boys laughed and laughed.

"Yeah," said Harold, "he could fight with *Wedgie Power*!"

George and Harold spent entire afternoons writing and drawing the comic adventures of Captain Underpants. He was their coolest superhero ever!

Luckily for the boys, the secretary at Jerome Horwitz Elementary School was much too busy to keep an eye on the copy machine. So whenever they got a chance, Harold and George would sneak into the office and run off several hundred copies of their latest Captain Underpants adventure.

After school, they sold their homemade comics on the playground for 50¢ each.

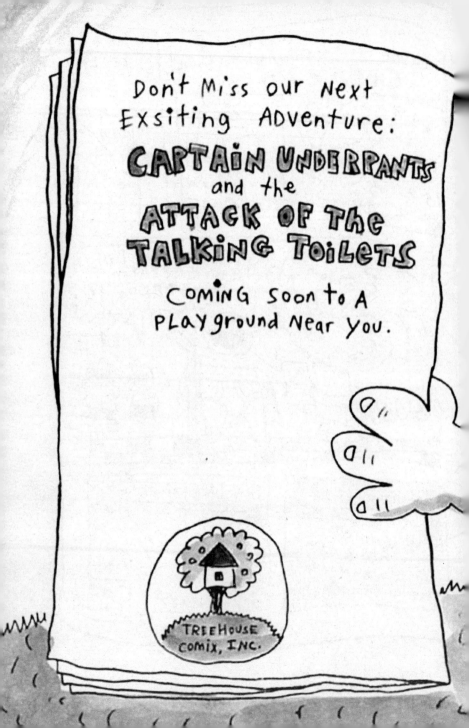

CHAPTER 4

MEAN OLD MR. KRUPP

Do you see that old guy
looking out the window
up there?
That's Mr. Krupp,
the principal.

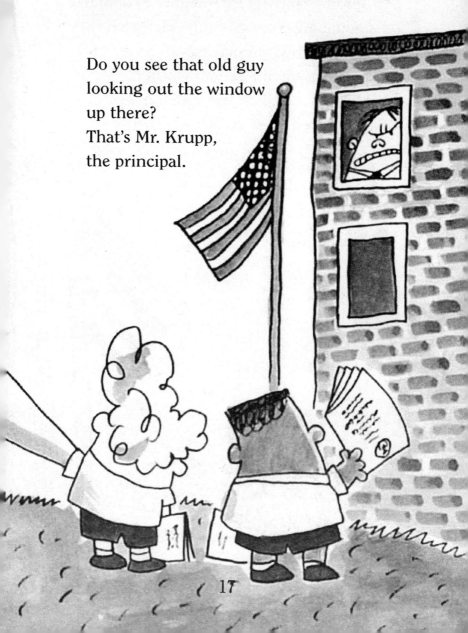

17

Now, Mr. Krupp was the meanest, sourest old principal in the whole history of Jerome Horwitz Elementary School. He hated laughter and singing. He hated the sounds of children playing at recess. In fact, he hated children altogether!

And guess which two children Mr. Krupp hated most of all?

If you guessed George and Harold, you're right! Mr. Krupp *hated* George and Harold.

He hated their pranks and their wise-cracks. He hated their silly attitudes and their constant giggling. And he especially hated those awful *Captain Underpants* comic books.

"I'm going to get those boys one day," Mr. Krupp vowed. "One day very, very soon!"

CHAPTER 5

ONE DAY VERY, VERY SOON

Remember when I said that George and Harold's "silly streak" got them into big, *BIG* trouble once? Well, this is the story of how that happened. And how some huge pranks (and a little blackmail) turned their principal into the coolest superhero of all time.

It was the day of the big football game between the Horwitz Knuckleheads and the Stubinville Stinkbugs. The bleachers were filled with fans.

The cheerleaders ran onto the field and shook their pom-poms over their heads.

A fine black dust drifted out of their pom-poms and settled all around them.

"Gimme a K!" shouted the cheer-leaders.

"*K !*" repeated the fans.

"Gimme an N!" shouted the cheer-leaders.

"*N !*" repeated the fans.

"Gimme an . . . a-ah-ah-A-CHOO!" sneezed the cheerleaders.

"*A-ah-ah-A-CHOO!*" repeated the fans.

The cheerleaders sneezed and sneezed and sneezed some more. They couldn't stop sneezing.

"Hey!" shouted a fan in the bleachers. "Somebody sprinkled black pepper into the cheerleaders' pom-poms!"

"I wonder who did that?" asked another fan.

The cheerleaders stumbled off the field, sneezing and dripping with mucus, as the marching band members took their places.

But when the band began to play, steady streams of bubbles began blowing out of their instruments! Bubbles were *everywhere*! Up and down the field the marching band slipped and slid, leaving behind a thick trail of wet, bubbly foam.

"Hey!" shouted a fan in the bleachers. "Somebody poured bubble bath into the marching band's instruments!"

"I wonder who did that?" asked another fan.

Soon, the football teams took the field. The Knuckleheads kicked the ball. Up, up, up went the ball. Higher and higher it went. The ball sailed into the clouds and kept right on going until nobody could see it anymore.

"Hey!" shouted a fan in the bleachers. "Somebody filled the game ball with *helium*!"

"I wonder who did that?" asked another fan.

But the missing ball didn't make any
difference because at that moment, the
Knuckleheads were rolling around the
field, scratching and itching like crazy.

"Hey!" shouted the coach. "Somebody
replaced our Deep-Heating Muscle Rub
Lotion with Mr. Prankster's Extra-Scratchy
Itching Cream!"

"We wonder who did that?!" shouted the
fans in the bleachers.

The whole afternoon went on much the same way, with people shouting everything from "Hey, somebody put Sea-Monkeys in the lemonade!" to "Hey, somebody glued all the bathroom doors shut!"

Before long, most of the fans in the bleachers had gotten up and left. The big game had been forfeited, and everyone in the entire school was *miserable*.

Everyone, that is, except for two giggling boys crouching in the shadows beneath the bleachers.

"Those were our best pranks yet!" laughed Harold.

"Yep," chuckled George, "they'll be hard to top, that's for sure."

"I just hope we don't get busted for this," said Harold.

"Don't worry," said George. "We covered our tracks really well. There's *no way* we'll get busted!"

CHAPTER 6
BUSTED

The next day at school, an announcement came over the loudspeakers.

"George Beard and Harold Hutchins, please report to Principal Krupp's office at once."

"Uh-oh!" said Harold. "I don't like the sound of *that*!"

"Don't worry," said George. "They can't prove anything!"

George and Harold entered Principal Krupp's office and sat down on the chairs in front of his desk. The two boys had been in this office together countless times before, but this time was different. Mr. Krupp was *smiling*. As long as George and Harold had known Mr. Krupp, they had never, *ever* seen him smile. Mr. Krupp knew something.

"I didn't see you boys at the big game yesterday," said Mr. Krupp.

"Uh, no," said George. "We weren't feeling well."

"Y-Y-Yeah," Harold stammered nervously. "W-W-We went home."

"Aw, that's too bad," said Principal Krupp. "You boys missed a good game."

George and Harold quickly glanced at each other, gulped, and tried hard not to look guilty.

"Lucky for you, I have a videotape of the whole thing," Mr. Krupp said. He turned on the television in the corner and pressed the play button on the VCR.

A black-and-white image appeared on the TV screen. It was an overhead shot of George and Harold sprinkling pepper into the cheerleaders' pom-poms. Next came a shot of George and Harold pouring liquid bubble bath into the marching band's instruments.

"How do you like the *pre-game show*?" asked Mr. Krupp with a devilish grin.

George eyed the television screen in terror. He couldn't answer. Harold's eyes were glued to the floor. He couldn't look.

The tape went on and on, revealing all of George and Harold's "behind the scenes" antics. By now, both boys were eyeing the floor, squirming nervously, and dripping with sweat.

Mr. Krupp turned off the TV.

"You know," he said, "ever since you boys came to this school, it's been one prank after another. First you put dissected frogs in the Jell-O salad at the parent-teacher banquet. Then you made it snow in the cafeteria. Then you rigged all the intercoms so they played "Weird Al" Yankovic songs *full blast* for six hours straight.

"For *four long years* you two have been running amok in this school, and I've never been able to prove anything— until now!"

Mr. Krupp held the videotape in his hand. "I took the liberty of installing tiny video surveillance cameras all around the school. I knew I'd catch you two in the act one day. I just didn't know it would be *so easy*!"

CHAPTER 7

A LITTLE BLACKMAIL

Mr. Krupp sat back in his chair and chuckled to himself for a long, long time. Finally, George got up the courage to speak.

"W-What are you going to do with that tape?" he said.

"I thought you'd never ask," laughed Principal Krupp.

35

"I've thought long and hard about what to do with this tape," Mr. Krupp said. "At first, I thought I'd send copies to your parents."

The boys swallowed hard and sank deeply into their chairs.

"Then I thought I might send a copy to the school board," Mr. Krupp continued. "I could get you both *expelled* for this!"

The boys swallowed harder and sank deeper into their chairs.

"Finally, I came to a decision," Mr. Krupp concluded. "I think the football team would be very curious to find out just *who* was responsible for yesterday's fiasco. I think I'll send a copy to them!"

George and Harold leaped out of their chairs and fell to their knees.

"No!" cried George. "You can't do that. They'll *kill* us!"

"Yeah," begged Harold, "they'll kill us every day for the rest of our lives!"

Mr. Krupp laughed and laughed.

"Please have mercy," the boys cried. "We'll do anything!"

"Anything?" asked Principal Krupp with delight. He reached into his desk, pulled out a list of demands, and tossed it at the boys. "If you don't want to be *dead as long as you live*, you'll follow these rules *exactly*!"

RULES

KNEEL HERE

George and Harold carefully looked over the list.

"This . . . this is blackmail!" said George.

"Call it what you like," Principal Krupp snapped, "but if you two don't follow that list *exactly*, then this tape becomes the property of the Horwitz Knuckleheads!"

CHAPTER 8
CRIME AND PUNISHMENT

At six o'clock the next morning, George and Harold dragged themselves out of bed, walked over to Mr. Krupp's house, and began washing his car.

Then, while Harold scrubbed the tires, George roamed around the yard pulling up all the weeds and crabgrass he could find. Afterward, they cleaned the gutters and washed all the windows on Mr. Krupp's house.

At school, George and Harold sat up straight, listened carefully, and spoke only when spoken to. They didn't tell jokes, they didn't pull pranks—they didn't even smile.

Their teacher kept pinching herself. "I just *know* this is a dream," she said.

At lunch, the two boys vacuumed
Mr. Krupp's office, shined his shoes,
and polished his desktop. At recess, they
clipped his fingernails and ironed his tie.

Each spare moment in the boys' daily
schedule was spent catering to Mr.
Krupp's every whim.

After school, George and Harold mowed Mr. Krupp's lawn, tended his garden, and began painting the front of his house. At sunset, Mr. Krupp came outside and handed each boy a stack of books.

"Gentlemen," he said, "I've asked your teachers to give you *both* extra homework. Now go home, study hard, and I'll see you back here at six o'clock tomorrow morning. We've got a busy day ahead of us."

"Thank you, sir," moaned the two boys.

George and Harold walked home dead tired.

"Man, this was the worst day of my entire life," said George.

"Don't worry," said Harold. "We only have to do this for eight more years. Then we can move away to some far-off land where they'll never find us. Maybe Antarctica."

"I've got a better idea," said George.

He took a piece of paper out of his
pocket and handed it to Harold. It was an
old magazine ad for the 3-D Hypno-Ring.

"How's *this* going to help us?" asked
Harold.

"All we gotta do is hypnotize Mr.
Krupp," said George. "We'll make him
give us the video and forget this whole
mess ever happened."

"That's a great idea!" said Harold. "And
the best part is we only have to wait four-
to-six weeks for delivery!"

CHAPTER 9

FOUR-TO-SIX WEEKS LATER

After four-to-six weeks of backbreaking slave labor, grueling homework assignments, and humiliating good behavior at school, a package arrived in George's mailbox from the Li'l Wiseguy Novelty Company.

It was the 3-D Hypno-Ring.

"Hallelujah!" cried George. "It's everything I ever hoped for!"

"Let me see, let me see," said Harold.

"Don't look directly at it," warned George. "You don't want to get hypnotized, do you?"

"Do you really think it will work?" asked Harold. "Do you really think we can 'amaze our friends, control our enemies, and take over the world' just like the ad says?"

"It better work," said George. "Or else we just wasted four whole bucks!"

CHAPTER 10
THE 3-D HYPNO-RING

The next morning, George and Harold
didn't arrive early at Mr. Krupp's house
to wash his car and reshingle his roof. In
fact, they were even a little late getting to
school.

When they finally showed up, Mr.
Krupp was standing at the front door
waiting for them. And boy, was he *mad*!

Mr. Krupp escorted the boys into his office and slammed the door.

"All right, where were you two this morning?" he growled.

"We wanted to come over to your house," said George, "but we were busy trying to figure out the secret of this *ring*."

"What ring?" snapped Mr. Krupp.

George held up his hand and showed the ring to Principal Krupp.

"It's got one of those weird patterns on it," said Harold. "If you stare at it long enough, a picture appears."

"Well, hold it still," snarled Mr. Krupp. "I can't see the darn thing!"

"I have to move it back and forth," said George, "or else it won't work."

Mr. Krupp's eyes followed the ring back and forth, back and forth, back and forth, and back and forth.

"You have to stare deeper into the ring," said Harold. "Deeper . . . deeeper . . . deeeeper . . . deeeeeeeeeper."

"You are getting sleepy," said George. "Veeeeery sleeeeeeeeeepy."

Mr. Krupp's eyelids began to droop. "I'mmmsssoooosssleeepy," he mumbled.

After a few minutes, Mr. Krupp's eyes were closed tight, and he began to snore.

"You are under our spell," said George. "When I snap my fingers, you will obey our every command!"

Snap!

"Iwwilllloobeyyy," mumbled Mr. Krupp.

"All right," said George. "Have you still
got that videotape of me and Harold?"

"Yeeessss," mumbled Mr. Krupp.

"Well, hand it over, bub," George
instructed.

Mr. Krupp unlocked a large file cabinet
and opened the bottom drawer. He
reached in and handed George the videotape. George stuffed it into his backpack.

Harold took a *different* video out of his
backpack and put it into the file cabinet.

"What's that video?" asked George.

"It's one of my little sister's old
'Boomer the Purple Dragon Sing-A-Long'
videos."

"Nice touch," said George.

50

CHAPTER 11

FUN WITH HYPNOSIS

When Harold bent down to close the file cabinet, he took a quick look inside.

"Whoa!" he cried. "Look at all the stuff in here!"

The file cabinet was filled with everything Mr. Krupp had taken away from the boys over the years. There were slingshots, whoopee cushions, skateboards, fake doggy doo-doo—you name it, it was in there.

"Look at this!" cried George. "A big stack of *Captain Underpants* comics!"

"He's got every issue!" said Harold.

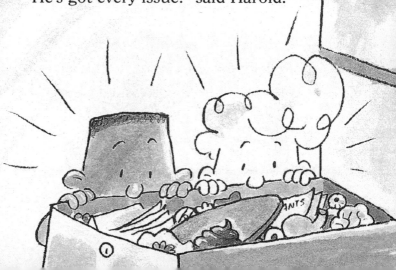

For hours, the two boys sat on the floor laughing and reading their comics. Finally, George looked up at the clock.

"Yikes!" he said. "It's almost lunchtime! We better clean up this mess and get to class."

The boys looked up at their principal, who had been standing behind them in a trance all morning.

"Gee, I almost forgot about Mr. Krupp," said Harold. "What should we do with him?"

"Do you want to have some fun?" asked George.

"Why not?" said Harold. "I haven't had *any* fun in the last four-to-six weeks!"